ANIMAL HISTORIES

Jerrod E. Bohn

Published by Unsolicited Press
www.unsolicitedpress.com
Copyright © 2017 Jerrod E. Bohn
All Rights Reserved.
Unsolicited Press Books are distributed to the trade by
Ingram.
Art: In-house artist
ISBN-13:978-1-947021-04-4

Many thanks to the following journals for first publishing some of these poems: *Commas & Colons, Phoebe, Bank-Heavy Press, Birds Piled Loosely, Word For/Word, Frank Martin Review, Emerge Literary Journal, Souvenir, Spry, FRiGG, SPECs, The Watershed Review* and *Smoking Glue Gun*. Additionally, all of CYCLE TWO originally appeared as a nonfiction lyric essay in *murmurations*.

I am indebted to the following writers whose ideas have informed these works: George Oppen, Dan Beachy-Quick, Daniel Heller-Roazen, Lewis Hyde, Allan Grossman & Mark Halliday, Nick Cave, Julia Kristeva, Sasha Steensen, Matthew Cooperman, Ronald Johnson. Also to Matthew Antonio, Chris Klingbeil, Ryann Peats and Gus Mircos, who read and commented on previous versions of these poems. Finally, to my mother and father, to whom this book is dedicated.

Contents

"...if a man ceases to think of himself as a part of history he must think of himself on the same plane as other animals."

—George Oppen (*Daybook III*)

CYCLE ONE—WINTER GESTATIONS (Our Memoried Wounds)

"It is because my mother is the remnant, the last person who, if she would speak, could know the name of that people who I over and over again in poetry invite to name themselves, so that I will know my own name."

—Allen Grossman to Mark Halliday (*The Winter Conversations*)

we have on display a nascent child

He eats his name as soon as he learns
his name is graspable but not as song
his belly forever eats his tongue

we once considered excising his skin
but composed entirely of knuckles,
he beat time on his own legs & stepped into
a circumcised world counting syllables
back into a voiceless O

he kept slipping between our fingers

now we keep him behind glass, his wounds
fill as soon as they become visible
he birthed himself a fleshless void.

He speaks through himself without
asking, but not full,
sings of a collapsed world

his hollow belly digesting his bones.

under the scalpel, the nascent child is a waiting ear

A tone to join the tongue in summit
nameless, though through its ascension
a howl to name his breath, the child
forgets his own condition.

Floors & rooms remember limbs,
having devoured himself, his body
confounds spatial relations, projects

into dust bipolar resonances of what
rupture recalls an act of speaking

nascent throats necessitating
their own demise.

His mother tore his larynx each time
she spoke so he forgot the apparatus,
leaving it with the other glyphs
lining her uterine wall

particular ascension
each eye is a wakeful tear.

handbook of parallel days: a nascent child's
primer

Behave as if your first memorable encounter
is of lacerating your own skin with brambles:

an act that does not make flesh the abstract
of pain, the definition rather names a particular
thorn as its own form of harm

do not make a habit of howling

your own name in your own presence
alone as when half-asleep an apparition
appeared & you couldn't move so you called
what you thought it was, its substance.

The fate of utterance is to be erased
with an airy scalpel for excising what you don't
love from what you do

remember they return & are spoken

repeat after us—new drawn blood
never dries in the same shape, always
scabs to silence the wound.

an indefinite remembered, the nascent child
recognizes himself

His cheeks began to become visible
looking into the mirror, he devoured
our reflections until alone in the room
digested the wildness of his tongue

beat fists in an orgy on floor tiles
rolled into a ball his foreskin
pulled up to plug both ears

we decided to show him his mother,
her womb that contorted his face
into one eye that violation's

ruining now opened to the sighted song
blasting through to his mouth's wholeness
the shattered glass that replaces "father"
his first surrogate word.

lullaby for a nascent child: the mind is always its
own neighbor

Hang on to the parable you
descended from milk

your mother's birthright
embroidered in skin

always greeting in dead letters,
your mouth spanning her nipple

invents suckled narratives
forgotten lyric

the nascent child's face presupposes its own
architecture

Self saturates self so we can't be
sure that even the tree growing
out of the sidewalk knows it is
providing its name to his mouth

necessary musicality, he makes
sound so as to sing a sprout
always already there

or if misspoken the tree's limit
bursts before him, who so burns
his bristling skin

words heard within his mother's womb
come to be through his ears a fissure

each principle of form, the artery
by which he walks, his throat breaking
music's necessity, so as to sing
to the wilted being of the tree.

handbook of parallel days: the things don't know
their names

We have in abundance oratories that reek
solipsistic, like how you clutched your toes
to verify a touch other than your mother's

you betrayed sound before speaking

hands are, we cannot deny, named material
we see the sun cradle itself, the infant mimics
the maw whose wounding stops her song

abundantly you ask for bread,
convincing your belly full
though we know not what fills it,

a note echoed when light first becomes eye
becomes your infant-garble declaring

I am now outside the wound.

a babbling body, the nascent child is always
suspended between rooms

Why do we beg of his eyes a child
we saw dusting his hands into earth
breath reaching a white line that isn't
the visible juncture as through a wound

bodies part ways at fracture
returning to words they sleep
as he sleeps, calling himself
to eat of the earth is to watch worlds

disappearing near his eyelid we forget
how words form our separate bodies
being his eyelid whose dust is children

did sight precede song or is seeing
prior to spoken touch a juncture
visible our mouthful of dust.

the nascent child realizes it is howling through a
collective wound

We do not mean the absence of a name
giving our hand to him we thought

he'd see how fingers form a formless world,
fitting a sun into a thumb, this erasure

creates a hunger that can only swallow itself.
His mother, a remnant of his still-

birth his hollow belly can only crave
can only devour a half-sung womb.

the nascent child charts itself as beyond a hunger

Swing treble low leaves full of breath
that in the aphasiac mouth build double
needs for lyres, like meat roasting over a spit

infant-tower, a single babble left
abandoned before the pyre of cool embers
rubbed into the forehead, scooped out

strung phylacteries, the song is always
its own reason for asking

unuttered desires sublimate in the belly,
hollow in letters, hemorrhaged harmony.

handbook of parallel days: the infinite room holds
its own sound

We cry out to dispel archetype
our nativities are always a custom for meandering
airy hallways that pronounce breath
so themselves are

menageries of birth turned light
palliative spirit, your crowning mind
speaks first of entrance

later your slurred tongues' processions
come guided by a first letter
that through a wound allows your utterance

always already forgotten.

lullaby for a nascent child: head-blow predicts the
grafted tongue

We met you in echo
smudged outline in waves

cautious of cracks breaking
your mother into veins

we spoke that static,
& you became static

because before you, a singer
wounded you with her hymn

examined through glass, the nascent child knows
his mouth is an infinite room

We mistook his words for fire

his shadow, drying perspiration
pooled on the surface; to drink
is to form the reflection into a picture

sometimes there are no signs for fissures

say blue, & the elbow becomes sky
breaking sound into arable
fingers that know each limit

to be a sound note transparency

the forgetful microscope names
him the next patient before settling
as each eye rounds a ruptured line.

handbook of parallel days: the poem compels its
own loneliness

We called you a window because we forgot
how to arrive, so in parting our voice
came closest to transfiguring shadows
cast blue across your body a wall

with rearranged barriers, this metonymy, we name
your flesh coming full out of a portal

an entrance every word composed of I
of O written on sheets recalls

our otherwise selves metamorphosed into
arrivals not of sound which is why when
we speak you, we blow through you
remnants of what never could be said.

whatever the invisibles demand: the nascent child
comes of age

Of or being concerned with a hand,
caught in the act of retrieving
your exiled tongues erased as spoken,
as though sounding from mountains
storm-bearing winds

we have heard the sibilant, we have
breath that catches in our throat
like coughing or heaving some word
bound to fall out of this line

to pronounce at once remembers & forgets
how we speak is already a boundary
between what was never said & what will never be;
it's why we prefer to forget your name

held hostage, our mouth better banished
and your forced withdrawal brings you closer
to hearing inaudible alphabets,

bushes that only look like they're on fire
bordering the inevitable gale.

CYCLE TWO: GRAFTING A TONGUE (An Animal History)

"...for the love song is the light of God, deep down, blasting through our wounds."

Nick Cave (*The Secret Life of the Love Song)*

Invocation

This seeing is as of memory. I am avoiding you as I am avoiding poetry. I am sleeping in until my body's prose can't bend a line a line a line. There is no other tongue. I rise inaudible because my rest is a sentence, or has sentenced my rest to a state of making sense. The day is inaudible, still blusters with sound. I am a poet of dusk. In non-dusk—I, the mute prophet, singing hymns in a wild blur of inarticulation. in the language of gods no longer sung. What of this? You stretch your legs long & I shout horrors like departures of pigeons, I want it to! I want it, too. I penetrate, penetrate, I penetrate but I divide. I can't not split apart while thinking of the essential function of the word divorced from its tonality. In scatters of swallows from their drowsy nests the word lives without tune. Why I can't. Why I lip-mime even a partial melody. You spread your legs & I want it too, I want it too, but night knows no flats, no clefs. Gutter-birds blare early. If that center has music in it, I will pour salt on the sleeping dead. Still words housed in the cradles of infant gods. I want it to. A poem writhes in the beak of dawn, destined for hellmouths. There is no other place for our marriage bed, these bloody sheets. These feathers. Among waving reeds & pines, rocked to sleep by a rose turned lullaby. Dismembered note from note. Arranged into treeline & horizon bridging day-sign from night-song. Therein, our poem.

I

The cat sits idle on its scratching post, licking its paws.
The cat looks at you with peacock eyes. The cat - its
own idol. You color a lung on a magazine ad. Maybe
People. Some celeb shows poor fashion taste on the
opposite & you blacken the lung & ink in the motion
waves like a blood eagle. The cat still perches. Split-
orange mask & white booties. The cat, an ideal. You
add a big toe to the lung in the fashion of a beak & an
eyeball whose calico idol becomes the cat's first envy.
You long/lust for another celeb's Armani & black
North Face ski pants. The cat vomits a slimy tube of
hair & half-digested turkey Tuscany. On the window
shelf, an empty beer growler & a kachina with one leg
lifted as if corn might sprout from the magic markers in
the middle of your room. Or from the cat. Tail flicking.
Idle.

II

Some disturbance today in Facebook's failure to load
its chat feature. Forced to make face-to-face
conversations. You could talk to the calico, but she
licks litter dust from her paws so that her words reek of
fecal matter. You could always whoop at the
SportsCenter Top 10 plays but such hollering reminds
you of your father who after all these years talks to
phantom superstars, like your mother's half-smile.
There is, of course, your neighbor who has one good
dog one bad dog that follows you up & down the
sidewalk. Up & down the sidewalk. Up yipping, down
yapping, as you wonder if he likes antifreeze—not the
dog but your neighbor—because a dog's failure is not
unlike a child's—each one only trained or trick-prone
as discipline allows. You would pour antifreeze into
your laptop's USB port, yet a thimble holds better. But
why the fuck would your neighbor drink anything out
of a thimble? So you curse sewing needles and Isaac
Singer while stirring a little more brown sugar into your
coffee because after all, LeBron James does know how
to stroke it, & his game-winning grin is just for you.

III

You read an early morning text from an ex, apologizing for unfriending you on Facebook, which makes you think of another ex who wore a purple bikini & drank Dos Equis in your dream-imbedded dream. She stood near a farm pond with her bottoms pulled to one side so you could see one puckered labia. You thought about kissing her—your glowworm erection pushing into the down mattress—but when you made eye contact, you saw her pubic curls were ashy, though you remember them red, but you can't be too sure because you thought about porn stars while fucking her anyway. At any rate, she liked sex wrapped in the tiger blanket your parents gave you as a kid. She wanted it outside on the paint-peeled deck in plain view of the apartment courtyard. You obliged because you liked how she said your post-coital Camel was sexy. Smoke that pushed through your nostrils & dissipated like waking's hazy ache.

IV

A steak fat stain on the broiler plate suggests you need
to find a job. You scrub, but the green scratchy pad
only flakes like the default payment on your student
loans. The burnt marinade looks sparkly yet doesn't
quite bling. *Why don't you get a job?* you ask the cat as
you consider being her john because, after all, she's a
dirty whore who gives her arched-back purr to any open
hand. She'll do it for free is the only problem. So you
list your skills—Wii tennis champ—party-dip master—
can hold crow pose for seven breaths—and think about
how you once published a poem that a poet in
Pittsburgh might have seen while secretly compiling
your life's works into his own biography. *Fuck that guy*
you think, as you consider placing all your writing in
the oven, since lines melt like marbling. An ex told you
she'd never again date a poet. Her reasoning—you're
all words & give your love to everyone. When you said
you had yet to give your heart away, she replaced
"love" with "dick." You couldn't argue that point &
now wonder how a ribeye would look as an attachment
to your resume, but those in academia can't handle that
much meat. So you settle for a phallic smiley face next
to your prize-less name.

V

What's this? You—in another woman's bed? She's blissed & you're still awake recalling last night's topless teeth brushing & the aesthetic argument you had with her buckled thigh—European techno is only appropriate for dropping E in Ibiza while walking along the beach. You pull on your white t-shirt while considering the most non-cliché exit strategy—sneak down the hall in her Snuggie like a wraith. The calico's wrath awaits you. She'll follow from room to room meowing *fuck you, fuck you,* & it will sound like claws raked across a wipeboard. The woman next to you stirs & you think you could fling yourself from her window & float, like the expectation of touch on her now-exposed shoulders and breasts. Nipples self-asserting—*we have a soft spot for Garth Brooks.* Just when you can't stand to debate music with her anatomy any longer, she opens her eyes & you say *yes I'd love to stay for coffee & yes I'll have mine overeasy.* & yes, you both hear cheesy love songs when your fingers debate one another's smile lines.

VI

Despite knowing you shouldn't drink another high-gravity beer before meeting your friends out, you pop off another bottle cap & listen to five-second samples of songs you've considered downloading but haven't because you fear being ripped off. Like the time the cat brought you a legless cricket & tried to pass it off as an Eastern European delicacy. Or when you were ten & stuck in your childhood friend's vagina. She only knew where it went because a man with a beard taught her, & he had dirt caked under his fingernails like you. You ran home & washed your hands until the skin cracked & bled& you took a needle & pushed it under the nail-plate. Even today, you bite down to the quick if you see mud or oil or wing sauce hardened there. You consider pouring out a bit of beer for her, but no way she's dead because you heard she's married now & living in her parents' old house across from the rodeo arena where you chewed wild spearmint & then pecked each other's lips. Both of you looked at the holding chute, afraid you'd done something dirty. Something like whisker-burn. Like what you might hear if you actually listen to a whole song.

VII

Psychologists say some people hear two differing voices, & you can relate, though you prefer to picture them as two horses fused at the flank & pulling in opposite directions. Once you name Silly Horse, on account of the bizarre thoughts she makes you voice, while the other you call Banal. You've thought of severing them but are afraid they'd breed & birth more steeds to gallop up dust storms in your mind's pasture. Instead, you think of 101 uses for the cat in the event of a nuclear holocaust: rations scout, water pH measurer, your personal scratchy-tongued radiation remover & shoulder pet for you, the post-apocalyptic pirate. With matching eyepatches. The other horse says *brush the coffee stains off your teeth or the new woman's never going to kiss you!* & you say *haha horse* because you've explored her mouth, & other places. You now think there might be a third horse—a bluish-purple bronco with red eyes like two radio tower lights, only they don't blink & this horse neighs crazy., & when that happens, you imagine every object—even the trees—a conspiracy of hooves. So you ball your fists—each knuckle a reason unraveling some bark plot. The cottonwood in your backyard with the missile-silo trunk. A branch on the button. A branch parting its hair like a mane.

VIII

A lavender morning. Some French press & siphoned
songs off mix tapes you made with your exes. The one
that blushed on your moonlit balcony, trembling in a
blanket, shadowboxed above the courtyard menagerie.
This is where you made love. The one in Tennessee.
The one you drove back to Kansas. You'd like to credit
yourself for their culture, but truth is you stole from
their music libraries too so that if the calico's claws
caught on skin-fold & unraveled you, you would be
flesh of another's tunes. Are your songs in their little
toes or the grooves you touched? —each of them
lightening or pressing deeper in accordance to their
sighs? You trash them all. Each silver circle a relic of
bygone chords. For each you wail dirges—no—you
howl hymns of your own blessed discovery.

IX

Weary today because you stayed up late with the new woman customizing yourselves as monsters. You first chose fur over scales, but she suggested purple & blue plates with orange tips would better deflect rocks & bullets. Not everyone loves a monster. For a special power you opt for a pouch holding a smaller version of your monster-self who then has a pouch holding a smaller version of its monster-self & so on, like Russian dolls with fangs & claws. You also want a tail you can swing to clear out cars or sides of buildings. She wants horns. The calico kneads your thigh with clawless paws & you wonder if she remembers her claws' extractions, like how you chose to tear up cards from past lovers—not the paper but the words & how you took them. You wonder if there's a place for dead letters—not a holding bin but burial plot. What is afterlife to deceased sentiment? Maybe like reducing the self until nothing can be felt. Maybe like a squishy toe pad still tender from forced removal.

X

A day so desperate, even the coffee's brewed itself blacker. You reach into the couch cushions for small change but only find the calico's mangled toy mice, catnip intestines falling out. You wonder if money's to be made in small press ventures, so you brainstorm names on the back of last night's beer tab. *Rubber Chicken Tantra. Fetid Cat Publishing. The Martyrdom of St. Aloysius.* There's always the viral video option but what talent do you have? Folding your eyelids inside out? Karaoke singing emo/goth versions of lovey-dovey 60s songs? The market for that's tapped, you suppose, so you crunch the last of the fresh vegetables & wonder if celery ever feels slighted by carrot's success or whether tomato laughs at both of them. What the fuck did tomato do to get so rich & popular? The cat digs up a nickel from her litter box & sets it on the counter. You know she's been saving up for a green toy with a rotating laser light, so you appreciate her gesture. If only the microwave were a slot machine & chewed fingernails didn't seem so cheaply counterfeit.

XI

Your reading is interrupted by the heater's explosion,
like some intestine rapping on your door. Maybe to use
the cat box. Maybe the urinal like most adults do. You
aren't sure because you know to answer means you'll
have to shake its hand, & its shit won't rinse out of your
palm-prints for weeks. *Why don't you see who it is*—
you ask the calico but she's arch-backed. A balled fetus
of raised fur. So you return to your books, scribbling
notes in the margins like *that sounds like a goose bump*
or *aren't all poems nipples engorged*? But the pipes
keep rattling, plugged up to the bowels. Its movement
sloshy like it drank too much booze. You can relate
because last night you puked all over the sheets & slept
there like some marginal comment overlapping the
printed type. Vomited rice noodles, a narrative
counterpointed by pho-broth & PBR. Another page
annotated. BOOM! It goes again & you throw yourself
over the startled cat, afraid diarrhea will foam from the
vent & seep through the door-crease like the mid-
morning night you overslept. The last comment you
wrote on finishing the book—*my work is better—I'm
better than this.*

XII

Neck-crick & shoulder tightness indicate you slept
drunk again. Your hair pressed into the headboard so
that your earlobes dally on your collarbone. This only
intensifies your whiskey-beer-wine-tequila headache,
which drums like a fat Buddha's belly laugh. Your
breath is an arc welder. Your lymph nodes like cigarette
butt cans. The cat suggests yoga & rolls onto her back.
Paws extended toward your cheeks, uterine scar to the
ceiling. You decide she looks awkward so you get out
of bed & make elixirs from water & the dust particles
on your nightstand. Surely minerals. Electrolytes. Hell.
Sea Monkeys. This makes you laugh but you wince
because your frontal cortex pounds like a woodsman
log-chopping in glockenspiel din. You try green tea for
detox & the boiling water gurgles your bowels, so you
run to the shitter where it gets murky. You stare bare-
assed into the toilet. You can see chili flakes & the first
two digits of the phone number some other woman
wrote with her fingernail on a tongue-knotted cherry
stem. *I ate adobo sauce?* You wander while thinking,
right there in that turd-crack is a fissure or language. A
crevasse humming with initiation songs.

XIII

You tear the top sheet off the bed in a fit of wild mucus.
What you mistook as cat vomit is only bloodstain from
a knee-gash. The curb bit you when you fell on him.
Where you left him passed out & bleeding on church
steps. A morning bell peals from a steeple. The cat
won't even cuddle you, & when you petition, she
reminds you that she isn't your replacement for the
woman whose heart you battered with an empty bottle
of her own whiskey. Your fists fold over linen like
bleach-prayer. Torn skin forms a scab that holds your
wound like baptism. You remember age ten &tearing
one-inch circles in your palm-flesh because you
couldn't stop monkey barring. The fat nun with the
lozenge eyes & hair-lip ignored you, & only after you
wiped your grit-stained snot on her vestments did she
say *now you know one-eighth of Christ's suffering when
they drove rusted nails into his open hands*. Corporal
work of mercy: breaking up last night's fight. The
spiritual work left on he who started it. You wonder if
he still lies there splayed out like diced-for clothing.
Piss-stained Hawaiian shorts. Plastic-flower lei
unstrung. The saliva he spit out when your shoulder
drove into his chest, dried now across his cheeks.
Broken into barbs.

XIV

You read words on the undersides of your eyelids &
they spell your ex's name, which is longer than the
accepted terms for despair. The cat wrinkles her nose at
your suggestion of exercise so you split a Guinness—
yours as milk for Cinnamon Toast Crunch & hers as a
toast to her own idleness. Her disinterest is starting to
rub off on you. You sleep in late when you're not tired
because you have become so detached that every object
is beautiful. Even the blob of your post-binge drool
seems a purple orchid waiting for the bees crusted in
your eyes to pollinate it. This reduces you to
stammering & you understand why Kant never left his
hometown. Why Kant never masturbated. Because now
as you sit there jerking it to some first-timer getting ass-
fucked, all you can think about is how lovely she might
have looked in the blue afterglow of a thin, rainy
evening. The scene begins to border on the sublime.
You turn off the computer & dive under the sheets, &
try to love something so that you can make it through
your day, but even the pattern on the wool blanket has
symmetry like your ex's face. The monster you try to
imagine has her fingernails for eyes.

Invocation

Who would stop this buzzing? A small, terrible fly. Its wings beat impatience like the sun's insistence, & who makes the swat come down? A horrible action. All wrist, A splattered compound eye. I would nurse you like a child. Hold you to the swollen tit of my hand. These words are not enough to go by. They pass, making sunset a mockery. Not that dusk, but the remembrance of some other dusk when I wasn't your mother & my grandfather's veins weren't feeble as twigs. Who would stop that buzzing? The world is living under the rubbing of a fly's legs. We are flown on its back hairs. I sat in the forest by myself, pretending the pond scum had wings because it had to fly. Soar. Nothing is still. Being stationary is for writing long letters that nobody will read over a static moment of coffee & television. Who would stop buzzing? The hum's in the head of the earth's core & boils itself out by belching magma. Who among us is fit enough to walk the lava's scars & call oneself a husk born of flame? We are wilting in a slow embrace of arils. Who alone would stop the buzzing if it meant that all that's digested inside a fly's throat would go unvomited? Alone who? Who would quell some incessant din.

CYCLE THREE: GRAFTING A TONGUE
(Handbook of Parallel Days)

"…as if the sole place of poetry were in an indistinct region of speech in which memory and oblivion, writing and its effacement, could not clearly be told apart."

—Daniel Heller-Roazen (*Echolalias)*

to be read in accordance with today's testimony:

Enough batter in the bowl to leaven
idiolect, proportional to
curvature of the baking pan's mold

at 350 & twelve minutes, we have
bread to break the suspension
fixed between our noses

hosts of utterances come to mind
crumbs tumbling out of hand

mimicked in a gesture of swallowing
whole crusts which nourish
our mouths announce silences.

to be read after waking relieved to find that the
one beside you is not the one of whom you
dreamed:

To make fire, cool first
the songs echoing through the bower

our mouth, when multiplied,
makes double of two notes,
the embers resistant to discord

range of single voices
that shade trees occupy

in what divisions
do concordant flames settle hot,

knowable

shrill call of the swallow-tongue.

to be read before studying your head's impression
on the pillow:

A cold line arches across stilled sheets
morning breezes, a midge's weight
expectation of being uncovered, a light

left on in the kitchen kept watch overnight.
Coffee ground for tomorrow, so too plates
stained by eventual meals& the clicking of

a tongue; sleep functioned only to erase
yesterday's last thought, now hardened
crust, as it seeps from the sometimes eye,

malleable nearer nose-bridge, these memories
have a way of returning a midge to the first
form as if hovering off walls wet with rain.

to be read after crossing one's name off the guest
list:

Bridges not meant to be there,
a gulf swells to cover formalities.

Glasses clinking in a nearby room
voices coming out of white noise

television stations no longer air
in the dead hours when evening rain drips

static conversations, but somewhere,
laughter, though the channel is now impassable

connection between points A & B
is tangential to the open mouth-span.

to be read after the day's first sublimated impulse:

Two teeth tense the lower lip, others hidden,
a physical act to bind the finding

don't take cream or sugar, don't
care for prayer; a tethered dog

salivates the wrought iron fence
someone or nothing fixes a stare

to infinities of grass, while the blue
overhead empties our skin of skin.

Pen pulled out, idle stir-stick
words used to cover what's leashed;

god is a name for limited time
the sun sets aside for borrowing.

to be read after translating white noise into every
knowable tongue:

Tonight, a mutiny of stars.

Expect to see angels,
vast angular multitudes
borealis hailing the world

visible with its songs.

Nightbloom, only a cricket
searching for a mate;

the erasure of nothing
births a form we can know

if only we can touch it.
Can sing

the good news passing here
as sparrows rise
to the eye the

O to lip-
corners in gloria
in excelsis in.

to be read after gazing at an erotic photo of
someone to whom you didn't make love:

Machines swept the roads last night
clear of leaf-remnants so unimpeded

the moon walked over tar.
Vestiges of a dream wherein

androgynous rooms chose their sex,
neutered out of walls that turned

genitals inward to face the other,
asleep in a grafted bed;

brush-whir piling useless parts
into gutters, a decision to rise,

to forget nothing's tongue
touched brows & spoke thighs.

to be read during an operation that involves
excising the lyre grown under one's skin:

To become melody, carve the cochlea
into a hut so nerve impulses can break into
strings like shadows demanding names.

Let this slip into impending darkness
to see old languages reverberating off walls
into lines, forgetting how they are framed

dwelling in dispersal like ancient tongues,
where every myth is the color of red wine.

know this because god's teeth
are always in your mouth.

Creation is a grape we feed ourselves
to sew up our genitals

sound blaring from our memoried wounds

to be read after pulling out glass shards:

We can't hear longed-for notes
we don't have ears for them
we can't make mouths
but breath is there.

We dance, there is no breath
or ancestral residues. This loud hour

obliterates fossil memory of our mother
crying, we might leave her but we've already

spun the next song into silence; we have
what we lied about not having:

a mother whose humming we repeated,
in utero hummed the music, who even owns
the scars we sing to, origins
forgotten in light's first glimpse.

to be read when the entire assemblage recognizes
itself as a severance:

Whenever slough separates, skin must be
balmed & soothed so that the wound

has no memory or injury. It will return
prodigal, to stake claim over the body.

Incisions are essential to stitch as
each hand holds aloes or scalpels

day sheds itself of night-scars,
blasting through holes' whole returns.

to be read before replacing one's mouth:

Speak in unrhymed couplets & walk
as if grinding clay into casings, for ancestors

believe that you are a child. You
ceased being a child when your first
word was child, you were born
because once an infant god hungered.

your grandfather's green chair was
covered in fruit, but we did not have
names for calling as you sat
on his lap before you were born

out of blue rupture; every nascent throat
necessitates its own demise.

to be read before attempting to recreate the
previous day:

When breath is a stitch of swallows, when
touch is a parable of pigeons, when wings

leave their impressions inside elbows,
a single vulture becomes sheet music

caught in the blue-dawn mouth. A blur
of new distinction, the unfelt joint

pleats to pink-dressed wind. that morning
is a vestibule of crows come hymning,

the knuckle now felt, knuckle now
joined so as to sing harmonies of

starlings hemmed into a blackbird sun
of first melodies when breath becomes.

CYCLE FOUR: WINTER GESTATIONS (An Animal History)

"A home is never the world—a home is a separation from the world. A poem is never the world—a poem is a separation from the world."

—Dan Beachy-Quick (*Wonderful Investigations*)

I took a note out of the box. I read
its music. Between the bars, between
pints, glowed neon: humming, budding
light. the note's corners & clefs -
were avenues beating out flooded tempos,
burning in trash cans to keep warm. To keep
time I folded the note & pressed
my lips to its creases. I blew; I blew
until the sky blued out stars, deepest
nightscar now its own erasure heard
in tones this note this. Walking home
I strung guts of cat-faced forget-me-
knotted between wordpegs. I didn't
tune, I didn't read, just smashed the note
gathered its timbre its vibrations' kindling
burned. I warmed my hands to blue

long clouds wept low sky. I had a chisel
for memory. The term blurred like an edge,
tree-line high enough to doubt horizon ever
the face of someone never
a razor carving initials in rungs. Did I invent that
name? A term for seeing with clarity
divisions of aspen pine along ridgelines
so much sky sapping a resin or resonance
reason for memory. We cut distinctions
to validate our vision: the skin of someone
we maybe touched, the name ingrained
as freckles on an arm. Clouds, or their impressions,
felt as scabs: the barked-over remembrance.
I saw the branch whittle to a white point,
erased in blue. To question

you hold a branch to my head. You say
your name is. The branch shoots
stars like eyes, you say. Do not be
afraid. Your gown is a resin
or the resonance of hay between hooves.
I don't believe in mercy killing
unless the victim is half-buried in
theory. I want something I can feel,
like velveteen. I want something
felt, your pelvis caving in your
syllogism. You hold a reed to my mouth
& it won't go to my throat, no it
won't, though it smells like honey, like
your triangle. Your legs. I should
have murdered you with a thrust of
reason, but that unbinds us both. We are
chained to logic. Chains of chance
operations, victims of bees. Chants of

night voices sound like writing in convex
cloisters by candlelight, dreaming about
manuscripts illuminated to tell a story
that's just the chatter of crickets. I forgot
to open my notebook. I fit my body
against the walls & try to write as if
by cramping spaces I might compress
creation-marrow into my fingertips.
Whirrs of moonlight. Won't you read
how my father used to tell, not from books
his narrative of & in the land, told in ruffling
my hair. I'm not compact enough in this
space; the shower comes closest, my elbow
underneath my knee—two joints align.
The perfect poem. Mute stasis. Wind
can't breach the bathroom door. I shave
my head & write like flint rock. The hills

this line is an unnecessary bird whose chirping
instigates the poem. I chose this form because
I hungered to replace the voice I'd grown
accustomed to. Skin, the familiar sound
floating above still sheets: a wedded
sexuality. Clamoring to taste the throat,
the perverse bird who feeds its young its own
regurgitations. I sat up late rationalizing
famines that necessitate mercy killings.
This thought is a necessary line drawn
on the starling whose songs starts
 the spring whose return signals
hallucinatory April, whose hymn reeks
sparrows. When I was eight I recorded
my voice because I thought the cassette
might extract it. I played it back, its tone
avian & this I think this form alien

I failed to see through the glass. Even leaving
the glass left a watermark near a book
sitting on the glass table. I failed to see
my hand open the book I had forgotten
many times before. I failed at forgetting
your name in beads of water, your name
on my hand under the glass, under the book
table that is damp, outside rain in rings,
forget I said it. Your name. My failure
to empty the glass of the book's words
beading on the pages, seen as circular
stains in names, the rain rings audible,
forgetting. For getting. For giving myself
to writing your name in condensation
I fail in seeing. Through the glass, the book
leaves words ringing. My hand

a film appears over the projection screen
your body in mine—an ark. My father
used to hold me & sing the world into
being. Little baby elephants in his hands,
half-mad wolves in pairs. In pouring
the entire earth made flesh, the word
he whispered to the orb breathing in
his aftershave. My mother made
few covenants. Your fingers fewer
projecting familial promises, floating
like cork pieces your mother's wine.
I ignored those sounds you didn't say,
Sleeping, those oaths in distances between
our body, tossed on waves & broken
in their wake. Vow to always be; I am
not my father, I have no thumbs
cannot stop the flood or carry you
above water. Projecting

I give you a briefing—in the next room
they dance to hip hop & speak of passages
worded like wandering through vacuous halls:
I am not the man you loved. They stomp they
Slur. By dawn I will have passed out twice
two sips from most bottles: *I am a*
projection. I don't know what I'm projecting.
My spit glows in porch light, in your teeth
by morning, my knuckles now gashed;
they say I punched a bike & passed out twice
once as who you constructed. You were right
being afraid as they danced & we could hear
our lower lips detached from language: *I would*
that night was my shadow. A dim hum
shudders walls, the beat broken, trembling,
they ask if we're all right, we've passed out
beyond the frame containing us. As sound
will grow in memory, I reduce to

morning forestalls its arrival. Cement is stained,
name-dropping other months, aphids
eat the petals, pigeons shit wherever,
home is where the heart transplants
bread-crumbs in mouths of those
who name. The neighbor's lilacs must be
saved from tonight's late frost. Do we
have enough vases, enough faucets,
scented bathwater, the lavender oil
rubbed into your back, O
yes, the lilacs. I could not forgive
in calling have cut & bled let's return
do you find it odd I still speak
stems arranged in like broken glass
April's delayed departure. The full tub

sun-clot afternoon. A bandage fell
where I stopped reading, memorization
of the sequence: if the ant steps I will
crush & flush so much red light
contained beneath skin. Subtext is
what inches its way across floors;
are you understanding or should I
explain how bread crumbs have lost
absorbency? Those unread pages seep, and
we carry ten times our weight we can
never recall. Evening denotes a suture,
we can name what was said on the surface,
do you know evening connotes disjunction?
I remember poisoning the colony; it
wasn't a plot but some other mound; in
scars we seek relations. Sorry I forgot

expanses, dear, exist to fool the tongue. I don't
know why I still use these terms. It's been
one year & I can't picture your hip
jutting into the mattress, can't know
if we ever made love while candles cooled
on Saturdays. Dear, I mean, I must stop
inventing fishnets & knee-high boots
the arched sentence from neck-nape
to inner thigh. I must stop pondering
duplicitous acts of looking but not knowing
the name of; if it's my face, I did not
remember going to bed with crusted eyes. I
didn't mean, I just meant dear I am scaring
you, meaning to teach the consequence of
a gaze. The constant eye inhabits your spine,
&when it leaves, heat breaths the collar. You
will find me there, shared tongues parch
languages, dear. You don't have to

yes I am ordering you. Refrigerator magnets
arranged by advertised product, contents by
decomposing, we listened all night to air still
prayer. Yes get on your knees. Yes my belt-
buckle, hips & thighs. This is a catalogue of
obsessions placed into rows according to expiration
dates, we learned to ask the humming
don't let cold air escape. Don't do it
that way with so much teeth. Meals
we haven't made last Tuesday displaced
two summers ago my pants around my ankles
yes that's the way you out of sequence,
part my hair. the coffee mugs in rows
we had it out on the kitchen table last night
when air did still to a buzz of not for-
getting. Don't write reminders on wipe boards.
Do tongue them. Yes the light, door open, come

hill-memory betrays a truncated evening.
Took turns telling first how my father
described hoarfrost melting like cocoons
escaping fields; you never witnessed
this telling, so now I bear it. Your turn.
I prefer you naked. The expected dark
interrupted by sunburst, we scramble,
our bodies having talked all night
narratives in crusts near the eyes. Our
wounds can only endure so much
direct light before, out from wrinkles,
stories of how they formed. Patterns of
native grasses sparkling in beams. Silver
reflections of what we confessed
continue on each length of skin;
records I shouldn't keep, but need erased once
oceans cover this expanse. In dreams, waves

this morning sentences. I woke with my spine
aligned & swore the moon bisected my room's
diameter. I have no words to indicate
if this is important. When my father told stories,
moths flew out of his teeth. I stared
at his sleeves until they were whole
his stories. I don't want to get out of bed
because then I'll have to write. I'll have to scare
them & they'll eat through the screens. I have
determined the importance of lacking fresh
stories. I recycle my father's roots, a moth
flying parallel to dawn. Roll over the cold
side of the pillowcase eaten the gnash of wire;
I remember him telling the Pied Piper most:
what music will lure. I must get up.
Songs catch in my throat like wing flutter.
I import a memory. The parallax

late in rising counterword. Beds creaked
antithetical to dust slant the purring cat
the window. Tea kettle whistling. Did I?
How, when I'm still joining shadows into
separateness but yes, boiling water; my eyes
are still remembering to name. Without
curtains, the room looks reductive. I am;
I see. My hands grow large
I see the tea's herbal bitterness, without
fingers the taste fails these enlarged textures,
walls & how they smell. You, on pillow-
case, you, rising with my tongue between your
legs. This occurred months ago when tea
explicated how we woke constrained. This
isn't a sonnet, we've gone more lines,
witnessed air slack as lungs stopped breath's
blue flocks. Flown signs

vacant lines recede. In tall, after dark
embers I trace a leaf untouched by when
I try to sign in ash. It fills my throat, my limbs
bark over, I swore I heard you reduce to
hearing. In sight reduced. If I stare,
in sight the tongue becomes glyph:
too long fixed, & this I think is
memory. The picture, in fingerprints,
did it come from flame or mouth? My
native language fell out. The placenta
shadow gone, a white ellipse passes
these walls. You must read between this
allegory the lining of an open room, in
vein signs I sought in sight to spark,
lodged within an ear, gray dust forms which
we agree is contention. You sweep the image
itself names. Particles held

in smoke an inner-ear parable. My father, a burning
pasture, becomes a bare consequence for rain.
Can this be any more peculiar—me bellowing
so much dry wood they say it could burn until
inhaling campfire is all we can hear? Residual
sirens lure onlookers; I've always thought
them prettier when bound. To write risks
suffocating. Pentecost captured
my attention most Sundays by how, with burning
foreheads, the apostles spoke like gods. I don't
imagine words but glyphs, issuing from mouths:
idiot names spoken of in crackling
shadows. Light will choke the tongue, will
fix deities. We disciples sang embers to our
father. What is ash becomes a green world.
he smiled as he drove through smoke
sweat from his open beer can. A sprout

from sleep-echo, a rupture. I, breathing in,
forestalled quiet from just-washed linens
wrapped around my ankles, the poem I kept
 hidden but written in the sweat-halo
around my pillow. Have I remembered any
of my father's stories, recited to you as moths
rose & fell from your chest. My stories are
spoken in the same breath. Did I tell you wing-dust
makes possible the flight?. From my mouth,
tales unwind to bob above candles; from their
lips I recalled narratives but forgot them
to begin implies a middle. I still attend
your side of the bed though I am running
out of air. We reach this leg-bruised shin;
I fell last night though I always inhale, caught,
thus no conclusion. Or an empty

echo-bird elation. I thought about poems
I'll write in my middle-age as a father
who has no words for son so they sit reading
familiarity that bonds their silence. These
meditations have no depth, only narrative.
My thoughts of where we slept, how we fucked,
how I measured last night's absence, dreaming
skeletons out of branches, mooneye between.
They danced, ragged, as if I knew them.
Teeth tethered to the skyball, attending
anything with stuck stillness, which becomes another
term for love. This middle place disgusts
me. Who names their children after
fused tongues without relation, a metaphor
or nothing. My father tells one thing clear:
distance derives from proximity, he never
wrote.; he can't even Of sameness comes

About the Author

 Jerrod E. Bohn's work has appeared in *Phoebe, FRiGG, SPECs, Souvenir, Word For/Word, The Montreal Review* and several other publications. A graduate of Colorado State University's MFA program, he currently resides in Fort Collins where he teaches yoga and writing.